Fluffy Animals

BARRON'S

First edition for North America published in 2015
by Barron's Educational Series, Inc.

This is a Carlton book
Text, design, and illustrations
copyright © Carlton Books 2015

Published in 2015 by Carlton Books Limited,
an imprint of Carlton Publishing Group,
20 Mortimer Street, London WIT 3JW

All inquiries should be addressed to:
Barron's Educational Series, Inc.
250 Wireless Boulevard, Hauppauge, NY 11788
www.barronseduc.com

ISBN: 978-1-4380-0567-6
Date of Manufacture: December 2014
Manufactured by: Leo Paper, Heshan, China
Printed in China
9 8 7 6 5 4 3 2 1

Product conforms to all applicable CPSC and
CPSIA 2008 standards.
No lead or phthalate hazard.

Fluff and frolicking!

Are you ready for some fluffy fun? It's time to meet the cutest animals around! Say hello, then give these pals some sticker toys and treats.

Hello! My name is Sunny.

I'm Silvy. Purr-leased to meet you!

2

Find the stickers in the middle of the book

4

Woof, woof!

Inka and his friends are a noisy bunch! Say each of the sounds out loud, then stick the right animal picture in the frames.

Woof!

Neigh!

Meow!

Quack! Quack!

ANSWERS ON PAGE 64

Burrowing bunnies

Which hole is Rusty the rabbit going to pop out of next? Use your stickers to decide!

Find the stickers in the middle of the book

5

Find the stickers in the middle of the book

6

Clever pup

Inka can't wait to join his puppy agility class! Stick in cones for him to weave through and ladders for him to scamper up and down.

Cheer up, Betsy!

Betsy the bear cub is feeling lonely. Stick in some fluffy playmates for her to play with.

Find the stickers in the middle of the book

8

Rumbly tummies

The pets are getting hungry! Look at the shadow outlines,
then stick in the right food bowl for each one.

ANSWERS ON PAGE 64

Ready for walking

Inka the puppy is going out for a walk. Help him get ready by sticking on his leash and jacket.

Find the stickers in the middle of the book

9

Find the stickers in the middle of the book

10-11

Cute cat show

Look at this parade of purr-fect pussycats! Which one deserves to win a trophy? Stick the cup next to the most glamorous kitty, then give rosettes to the runners-up.

Happy pics

Wriggly Rusty can't sit still for the camera. Look at this cute photo of him! Now place the frame on the picture below that matches it exactly.

1

2

3

4

ANSWER ON PAGE 64

Billy goats fluff

This billy goat is very proud of his fluffy kids!
Fill his stall with even more adorable little goat babies.

13

Puppy postcard

Inka's owner has sent him a postcard. Can you help him decorate it?
Use stickers to make a delightful doggy scene!

Wish you were here

Horsing around

This meadow is full of frolicking foals! Stick some lucky horseshoes on the gate, then add lots of pretty flowers.

Find the stickers in the middle of the book

16–17

Farmyard fun

Inka and Sunny have come to the farm. Can you spot Sunny's six brothers and sisters? Put a cute chick sticker on top of each fluffy friend.

ANSWERS ON PAGE 64

16

A visit to the vet

The vet's patient is very small and very fluffy. Who could it be?
Stick a shy animal visitor in the carrier.

18

Cute collar

Inka needs a new charm for his collar. Would you choose one? Find a sticker you like, then put it in place.

Find the stickers in the middle of the book

19

19

Find the stickers in the middle of the book

Painted paws

Uh-oh! Who has walked through the wet paint?
Look at the tracks then stick the right animal
at the end of each trail.

?

?

?

ANSWERS ON PAGE 64

Egg-citing times

Mother Goose's eggs have hatched!
Stick four fluffy babies into the nest.

Find the stickers in the middle of the book

21

The perfect pet

Do you dream of having your own pet? What kind of animal would you like best? Stick a picture into the frame.

Animal parade!

Find the stickers in the middle of the book

23

The animal parade is in town! Look at the rows, then use stickers to decide which creature is missing.

1.

2.

3.

ANSWERS ON PAGE 64

23

Birthday bunny

Rusty rabbit is one today! All of his friends
have come to join the party. Decorate the scene,
then add a cake and presents.

Happy 1st Birthday

Pet shop problem

Find the stickers in the middle of the book

26

Abigail is choosing a guinea pig to play with.
She wants it to have curly, white fur and
blue eyes. Stick the cutie into her hands.

Dressed up doggy

Fifi the poodle is so glamorous!
Dress her up in pretty jewels and bows.

Find the stickers in the middle of the book

28-29

Bamboo for you

Kiki the panda has lost her cub. Can you help find her?
Stick paw prints along the right trail through the bamboo.

Start

28

Finish

ANSWER ON PAGE 64

29

Find the stickers in the middle of the book

30

Five shy mice

Five little mice live in this classroom. Look closely, then stick
a slice of cheese next to each one that you spot.

ANSWERS ON PAGE 64

Barks on the beach

Inka loves playing on the beach! Find some
new pet playmates to join the outdoor fun.

Pussycat puzzle

Find the stickers in the middle of the book

This quiz has made Silvy terribly confused! Can you help? Stick a pretty kitty next to every statement that is true. Put a ball of wool next to each false one.

	True	False
1. Cats purr when they are feeling hungry.	⭘	⭘
2. Cats are playful pets.	⭘	⭘
3. They aren't very good at seeing in the dark.	⭘	⭘
4. Cats are very clean.	⭘	⭘
5. Baby cats are called "kittens."	⭘	⭘
6. All cats love water.	⭘	⭘

ANSWERS ON PAGE 64

12

16-17

19

20

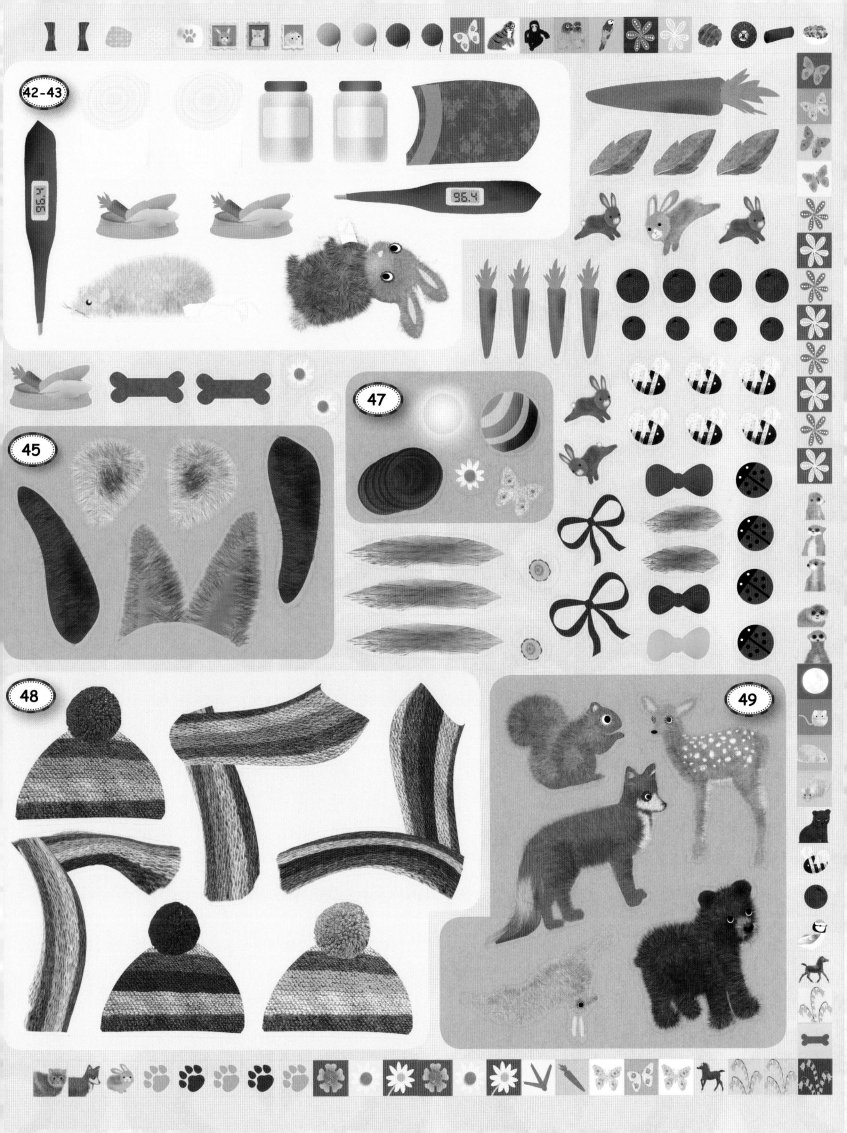

52

53

55

58-59

60

61

62-63

Penguin playtime

Look at these fluffy friends having fun in the snow!
Decorate their iceberg with snowflakes and icicles.
Then add some more playful penguins.

Find the stickers in the middle of the book

33

33

Monkey madness

Peer over the explorer's shoulder. Who can he spy having fun in the jungle today? Fill the trees with cheeky chimps!

Kitty colors

Silvy's favorite color is purple. Count up all the purple things on this page, then stick her picture next to the right number.

Find the stickers in the middle of the book

35

ANSWERS ON PAGE 64

4   5   6

Nighttime surprise

Did you know that some animals only come out at night?
Peep into the darkness, then stick the right creature
on top of each shadow.

Find the stickers
in the middle
of the book

36-37

ANSWERS ON
PAGE 64

Happy hamster

This baby hamster wants to get cozy in his cage. Use your stickers to make him a nice bed of straw.

Find the stickers in the middle of the book

38

Animal fashion

Find the stickers in the middle of the book 39

These puppy coats would look so pretty with some extra decoration! Use the stickers to design your own pet-tastic fashion.

Mucky duck

Oh dear! This little duckling has waddled right through a muddy puddle.
Stick some mud splats onto her fluffy feathers.

Mommies and babies

Baby animals are so adorable! Look at the mommy animals, then stick the right babies next to them.

Find the stickers in the middle of the book

41

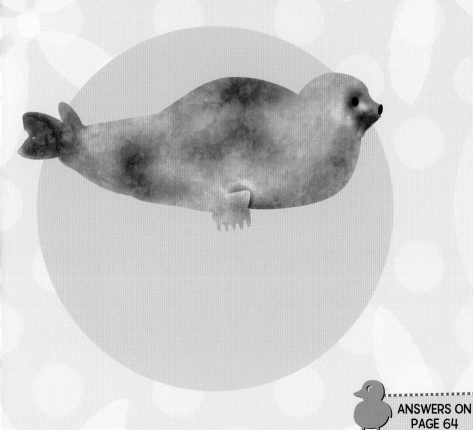

ANSWERS ON PAGE 64

Animal rescue center

There are lots of sad animals at the rescue center today.
Stick in some things to make them feel better.

Find the stickers in the middle of the book

42-43

43

Bunny cousins

Rusty comes from a big family. Lots of the rabbits in the meadow look just like him! Give them some juicy carrots, leaves, and berries to nibble on.

44

Laugh and listen

These happy animals are all missing something important – the right pair of ears! Use the stickers to finish off each pet portrait.

Find the stickers in the middle of the book

45

ANSWERS ON PAGE 64

Swishy tails

Popcorn the pony is getting ready for her first party.
Stick pretty ribbons in her mane and tail.

Puppy playground

Look carefully at these photos of Inka having fun at the park. Can you use your stickers to make the bottom picture match the one at the top?

Find the stickers in the middle of the book
47

ANSWERS ON PAGE 64

Chilly birdies

These cute baby owls sit on their branches all night long!
Stick in some little hats and scarves to keep them warm.

Find the stickers in the middle of the book

48

Forest hide-and-seek

Five animals are playing hide-and-seek in the woods today.
Stick the right creature on top of its hiding spot.

Find the stickers
in the middle
of the book

49

ANSWERS ON
PAGE 64

Paws and Claws Café

Sneak a peek through the windows of the
Paws and Claws Café—only animals are allowed! Stick
in some yummy food for the pets to nibble.

Find the stickers in the middle of the book

52

First swim

These little duckies are getting ready to go swimming for the first time! Give each one a shower cap to wear.

Odd-chick-out

Find the stickers in the middle of the book

53

Look at these pictures of Sunny in her henhouse. Which one is the odd-one-out? Make it look the same by putting a sticker over the difference.

a.

b.

c.

d.

ANSWER ON PAGE 64

Kennel cutie

Inka is moving into a brand new doghouse—peek inside!
Use your stickers to make it look bright and inviting.

Pussycat playtime

Silvy the kitten loves to play! Add some balls of wool for her to get tangled up in.

Find the stickers in the middle of the book

55

Animal expedition

Let's take a trek into the heart of the jungle!
Fill the leafy scene with even more fluffy friends.

Nibble and gnaw!

These little gerbils love to be busy! Fill their cage
with snacks, tunnels, and toys.

57

Lambs in the meadow

This field is full of frolicking lambs! Stick a little curly tail on each one, then add some pretty butterflies for them to chase after.

Find the stickers in the middle of the book

Meerkat madness

Who's that popping their heads out of the ground?
It's the meerkat family! Fill the scene with
even more meerkats!

Find the stickers in the middle of the book

60

Happy hamsters

This cute jigsaw picture has five holes in it!
Find the missing pieces and stick them in place.

Find the stickers in the middle of the book

61

ANSWERS ON PAGE 64

Find the stickers in the middle of the book
62-63

Sleep tight!

It's time for our fluffy friends to go to bed. Give Inka, Silvy, Rusty, and Sunny sleepy eyes, then add some fluffy mice.

Answers

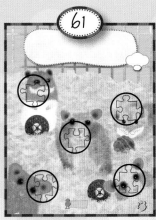